Knoxville Girl

ISBN: 1-4196-6297-X
ISBN-13: 978-1419662973

Visit www.booksurge.com to order additional copies.

BRUCE W. SPANGLER

KNOXVILLE GIRL

THE MAKING OF A PRESIDENT: A SMOKY MOUNTAIN VERSION BASED ON AND ADAPTED FROM THE BOOK OF RUTH

2007

Knoxville Girl

Also by the author:
The Gospel According to John Bill Bob Mark: A Smoky Mountain Version Based on and Adapted from the Gospel of Mark
2003

Reva Kathleen Franklin
October 9, 1911—September 1, 1953

Ruth's Pledge to Naomi

Do not press me to leave you
or to turn back from following you!
Where you go, I will go;
where you lodge, I will lodge;
your people shall be my people,
and your God my God.
Where you die, I will die—
there will I be buried.
May the LORD do thus and so to me,
and more as well,
if even death parts me from you!

Ruth 1:16-17

SACRED

Swiss researchers have discovered
that human tears are dripping
with serotonin.
It explains the calm
after the storm.
There's that fullness-
proof our grief is potent,
more that just salt.

But haven't we known it
forever?

Ancient Hebrews
collected their tears
in porcelain cups, guarding them
like jewels, treasure.
Those who had suffered
were esteemed.

When the crops failed and
the children were hungry,
their empty bellies protruding
into the dust,

when mothers lost their
sons, when sons became cruel, when
the red heat seared across
sweating shoulders, when all
that was left for hope
was the uncertainty of leaving,

the cups overflowed

Melanie Williams

To my hillbilly kin both known and unknown

I dedicate this book to my closet and loving kin,

Phyllis

Mom

Danny and Ammie

Justin

Tyler

Preston

Spencer

Bill and Keri

Rori

William

Tom and Linda

Mellony

Mallory

Patti and Mike

Beth

Tim

Katlin

McKenzie

Emily

Jacob

Bobby and Miranda

Heather

Johnathon

Brady

Sally

Susan

Aaron

Brent

Kristi

Sheriden

Jordan

Mother Pickell

Terry and Katherine

Brandon

Morgan

THE FIRST WORDS
A Smoky Mountain Version

A Smoky Mountain Version?

Yes, a Smoky Mountain Version.

My first book, *The Gospel According to John Bill Bob Mark: A Smoky Mountain Version Based on and Adapted from the Gospel of Mark*, was not without some serious critics and skeptics.

I don't know whether you were making fun of hillbillies or Jesus, came one indirect, and I assume, dismissal of my book.

Neither, I assure.

In many ways, that book and this one serve as avenues for me to claim my heritage, my heritage as a "hillbilly." Both works are confessions of my faith in the risen yet crucified Jesus as well.

Whereas the gospel of the living Jesus is a call for all to claim their heritage as sons and daughters of God, one cannot assume the realm of freedom without acknowledging the starting point of bondage and brokenness.

Far too many of us, hillbilly or not, forfeit the life and freedom God intends for us in this life. Our fear of freedom is often traded for a bowl of porridge for something "heavenly and beyond." We dilute the gospel to an Anthony Robbins version of self-centric "positive thinking" to escape from our real selves. We sacrifice life for an unrealized one imagined in and for the life to come.

Yet when Jesus proclaims abundant life as a promise, he does not say that I have to be "ten-toed" to know about it! In other words, I need not be *dead* to know and experience God's new life! God intends life for this life! A life, admittedly, that is lived between joy and grief.

In a world seduced by the numbing narcotics of alcohol, television, and entertainment, faith sometimes becomes another device or means to amuse us to death with "heavenly purposes." Such amusement inclines the believer to avoid the burden of "feeling" and compels the stifled heart to dry up and die of cardiac lethargy.

What we often seek to ignore or suppress is the reality of our common "brokenness," often called "falleness." The acceptance of our brokenness, forgiveness of our transgressions, and the possibility of transformation take an act of God's intervention of grace in our lives. God's grace acknowledges the reality of a life lived between joy and grief.

My first book and this work about Ruth are attempts at envisioning a faith that lives—hillbilly style.

My hope is that both books stand in stark contrast to the accepted saccharin-laced theology that masks the depressed and repressed denial of our common brokenness, a life lived between celebration and extreme disappointment.

A "hillbilly" gospel has plenty to say about life, all in the name of Jesus.

My maternal grandmother, Reva Kathleen Franklin, appears on the cover of *The Gospel According to John Bill Bob Mark.* She also subtly appears in the book as "Katie."

I never met her though.

My grandmother took her own life in "mid-stream." As a middle-age adult, she could tolerate life no longer. I wish she could have known of Jesus's freedom and joy in this life. Instead of the overwhelming agony of pain of her brokenness and the taking of life by her own hand, I just wish she could have known the power of loving life and living love of the risen Christ in and for this world!

The Jesus of the Smoky Mountain Version (SMV) is about God's chosen, who is not afraid of being "earthy" in his words, actions, and hopes. Jesus calls and challenges us to get our nose out of the sky and look amongst and in ourselves and live! He invites us to celebrate amid our disappointments, and to hide our disappointments in our celebrations.

What you are about to read is a Smoky Mountain Version of the Book of Ruth.

This version, however, lacks the mountain clichés and thick vernacular of my previous work. You will find, hopefully, this version a little easier to read.

But hold on.

I write with a purpose.

I write not to entertain but to challenge.

There are some funny lines in the text, or at least I think they are side-busters.

The challenge?

The challenge is in the story.

The Book of Ruth is a provocative and suggestive parable of God's transforming grace in and for this life.

It hints at the social and political power of sexuality in a time past but also a time present. I will not stray from those provocative and suggestive leanings.

The story of Ruth is about "outsiders" and "insiders."

Southern Appalachian culture is "clannish" in perspective and practice. Respectful of those known and guarded against those unknown, this propensity has both aided and impaired most of us. This, too, finds a place in my telling the story of a "Ruth" from southern Appalachia named "Jenny Sue."

The book of Ruth is a parable.

I believe that Ruth's story represents a countercultural testimony that challenges the demand and expectation that insists on God operating through and only through the "status quo."

Ruth raises a God-question among "status quo" Israelites.

Would God do something redemptive through a people that God has condemned through and by the sacred scriptures? The Moabites, from the Israelite perspective, warrant and deserve scorn, social ostrazation, and public yet refined humiliation.

Ruth may just be a spiritual lesson with political and social implications, in parable form, for and about "outsiders and insiders."

If a parable is a "narrative of an imagined event used to illustrate a moral or spiritual lesson,"[1] then *Knoxville Girl* is not only a good story; it has something to say about God.

With this book, I hope to convey and illustrate the gospel notion that any one of us can and has been used by God for good—for others, ourselves, and even creation itself.

In other words, no one is beyond redemption.

Moreover, if no one is beyond redemption, then it goes that God can redeem anyone. And God chooses whomever as an agent of redemption within the paradigm of the resurrected life in Jesus Christ. God can use anyone and anybody to do God's work of salvation. God's salvation is simply attending to our brokenness through an unyielding presence.

This is the plot of the parable called *Knoxville Girl.*

In typical southern Appalachian tradition, storytelling is not entertainment but an act of communication.

In my culture, a good story is better than television. The reason? The pictures are better.

A good tale is more relevant than the *New York Times.* Tall tales come from other places than New York City.

Moreover, a good "yarn" is even better than iced tea. It lasts longer in satisfying a thirst for meaning and belonging.

A storyteller worth his salt never lacks embellishment, nor is afraid of stretching the truth. A good storyteller will also insist, *I will tell it thirty different ways before I lie about it.*

Furthermore, a good story must begin with a story.

The following serves as the "introductory story" to my story of Ruth. Though fiction, it is based upon a sermon that I heard some years ago.

Guess Who is Coming to Dinner?

Dang!

Dang! I hate these kind of days!

These words, self-muttered, belong to James Robert, a.k.a. Jim Bob. Most know him as Dr. Robert. Only to the closest of relatives and childhood acquaintances is he Jim Bob.

Dang! I hate these kind of days! he repeats as he drives up the mountain road towards his old family farm, the home of his aged mother.

Dang! he repeats as he firmly raps his balled-up right fist on the steering wheel of his Lexus sedan. His thoughts carry him to his pending visit with his mamma.

Now don't get him wrong.

His dangs are not directed towards her.

He loves her.

He loves her more than life itself.

He loves her more than sliced bread.

Tomorrow, however, is Easter and he had promised that he would come up from Knoxville and attend church with her.

He casts his "dangs" at the church and its people.

He had disavowed the church—his home church—any church. He had made such a vow of disavowing long ago. The rantings and ravings of the mountain people in worship, at his home church of Sweet Potato Possum Holy Bible Methodist Church of Sweetbrier, seem far too bizarre, whimsical, contrived, and just "flat-out" freakish for his sophisticated taste!

However, now in his early fifties and a professor of philosophy at the University of Tennessee, Knoxville, he has never come "clean" with his mother about his "prejudicial sentiments against the anti-intellectual expression of such ecclesiastical foolishness."

That is university talk for "Somethin' is a'stankin' around here!"

He wants to say, *Momma, the church just doesn't make any sense to me anymore. It just doesn't have anything for me. It is total foolishness!* However, to be honest and frank with her, he confides and consoles himself, would absolutely break her heart. Such revelations would break her heart into fine little pieces, like the shattering of antique Wedgwood.

Dang! I hate this! he repeats to no one and to everyone in the darkness of his car, whose interior is black except for the dim "lightning bug" green coming from the dashboard.

I hate the shallowness and ignorance of it all! he says to himself, reflecting on his childhood experiences of the church.

By now, his dread of attending church with his momma in the morning has caused a rumbling and welling up in the pit of his stomach. The rumbling pleads for escape and release, but finds existence only as a bitter tang that edges forward from the back of his throat yet simply hangs there.

I can stomach the shallowness...even understand those piercing, sharp cries and despairing rants, he continues with his reflections. *But the meaningless is just beyond endurance!*

Dang! I hate these kind of days! he curses as he desperately searches the leather passenger seat to his right. His attempt to find his paperback Penguin edition of Nietzsche's *Thus Spoke Zarathustra* is more out of want than reality. He had intended to secretly read it during the church service and with plans to be free of his mother's awareness of doing so as well.

He wants the book.

Yet his search is useless.

He needs the book.

His frantic and agitated search is compensation for the knowledge and fact that he had actually left it on the kitchen table back at home, placing it there, when he kissed his wife and two young daughters good bye a couple of hours earlier.

It was as though the frantic search would correct and alter an intention that he had failed to complete.

His wife had suggested that it was long overdue for him to visit his mother. *She has been asking, if not pleading, with you to come up there. Be a brave boy and do it. The girls and I will miss you but we'll just have to manage. I'll plan a girl's day out....*

He admits to himself the knowledge and appreciation of a loving partner, who all too frequently seems to know more about him than he could ever willingly muster to know about himself.

Dang! he says to himself for the eleventh-teen time.

This morning I'll be preaching from John, chapter twenty, the country preacher announces as he stands behind the handcrafted, walnut-stained knotty soft pine of a pulpit.

I'll be preaching from the King James Version because it's the right and only Word of God. And if King James is good enough for the Jesus and Paul, then it's good enough for this ole hillbilly! he insists.

Amen! shouts a voice from amongst the congregation.

For James Robert, however, the noisy hum of the service and the chattering of clear and not so clear voices of the call and response fade into the background "elevator" music. Though present in body, his spirit is absent. His thoughts are elsewhere, visiting St. Nietzsche.

The first day of the week cometh Mary Magdalene early, when it was yet dark unto the seepucker, and seeth the stone taken away from the seepucker, the preacher reads coarsely and loudly.

The utterance of "seepucker" interrupts James Robert's tranquil visit to St. Nietzsche, just as the ringing and pinging sound of any elevator bell signals the arrival of the next floor.

John Robert focuses in on the preacher's reading of John, which continues. *Then she runneth and cometh to Simon Peter, and to the other disciple, whom Jesus loved, and saith unto 'em, They had taken away the Lord out of the seepucker, and we know not where they laid 'im.*

John Robert had read the Bible "kiver-to-kiver," as his mama says. Admittedly, though, "seepucker" is not a familiar biblical term.

He searches, frantically, around his pew to confiscate a Bible nearby. He finds one in the pew immediately behind him. He turns to John, chapter twenty.

In doing so, he receives a rather loving and affirming nod and broad beaming smile from his momma.

He returns the smile but keeps the nod to himself.

Reading the first verse under his breath, another grin begins to emerge on his somewhat red and rosy face. He tries to hide both the grin and sense of embarrassment.

He tries to hide the laughter from his mother.

He is embarrassed for both himself and for the preacher.

The embarrassment arises out of the knowledge that the preacher does not know how foolish he sounds, and the professor feels the embarrassment that he wishes the preacher would or could.

The first day of the week cometh Mary Magdalene, early, when it was yet dark, unto the sepulchre....

Good God! John Robert bemuses as he rereads the text to himself. Though totally composed outwardly, he is laughing hysterically within.

This is more entertaining than the Jerry Springer show or even TBN...I guess you can get s-e-e-p-u-c-k-e-r out of s-e-p-u-l-c-h-r-e...and just think.... I've driven all this way, given up a day with my family, to hear and see a "see-puckering" preacher! This is just what I was expecting! Dang it!

* * *

It is now a year later.

The phone rings at midnight.

James Robert's wife reaches for the phone out of habit.

It's for you, she offers.

*Brother...*the voice bellows, loudly and coarsely.

The voice is unmistakable.

"Brother Jim Bob," the voice continues.

This is Brother Carl, your mama's pracher. I hate to be the one to tell ya this but your mama ain't doin' goot. She is terribly sick. I'm here at her home with her and the doctor. Doc says your mama won't make it till daylight...I thought you needed to know...I'm sorry for the late hour but I'm more sorrier about your mama.

That's okay, James Robert assures him. *I'm glad you called. I'll leave within the hour. I'll be there just before daylight.*

As he drives up the mountain road, the gentle emergence of the new day's sunlight weaves its way through the tall pines, making for an oversized gray picket that caresses the winding mountain road.

Inside the house, James Robert finds the preacher sitting in a wooden frame caned chair beside the bed, the bed that once served as a place of birth.

Upon entering the room, the mountain preacher greets the son by a nod and a forced smile, followed by a strong, warm embrace.

While in the grasp of the Spirit-called and Spirit-educated preacher, the Harvard educated college professor hears a whispered announcement. For the moment, it is only worthy for a son's ear. Yet, it is destined to become an echo throughout the valley. *I'm so sorry. Your mama passed about fifteen minute ago. She now lays corpse. May God bless ya!*

The son goes to the bedside, bends over, gently and repeatedly kisses the cold skin of his mother's forehead with wet, sweet pecks of affection. Then he lovingly strokes her callused but manicured petite fingers. The son finds his place in the caned chair where the preacher had spent his all-night vigil..

The preacher slowly walks over to the other side of the room. A faint silhouette of the tall lean figure of the preacher is cast upon the opposing wall by the illuminating light of the mountain morning sun, which shines through the mullioned window.

*You know...*pausing for a moment, the parson starts.

It's your mama's fault that I am a pracher. It all started the first time I came to the church over twenty year ago. I came because I was curious, as curious as a ten-year-old can be. Your mama's smilin' and glowin' face was the first one I saw, and she was the first one to say somethin' to me. She told this little ragged and dirty hillbilly boy that Jesus done gone and loved him. With that, I was convinced it was so. I really didn't know that Jesus loved me so. But what convinced me was that you mama was so convinced that it was so!

Your mama axed me about my family and schoolin'. She kept her eye on me all these years. As I got older, she would axe me about family and work. She prayed with me and for me when I felt the tuggin' of God's callin' to preach. And when I was at odds with both the world and myself—when I was wrestlin' with demons bigger than life—she always reminded me that Jesus loved me and she did too.

*I know that I'm not the brightest bulb in the box, nor the bestest of preachers...*His voice lowers to an almost inaudible level. *But I do know that I could count on your mama's prayers and support every time I stood in the pulpit.*

Tears begin to trickle down the preacher's sun-blistered cheeks as he concludes with a quickly mustered burst of energy, completing his spontaneous eulogy. *I do know that your mama loved me and I loved her like a mama. She meant the world to me.*

Understand?

Now, I do know that Jesus loves me 'cause your mama and Jesus done convinced me that it is so. I'm just smart enough to believe 'em both...I just wanted you to know that, Jim Bob.

Frantically, Jim Bob searches for words that cannot be spoken. The words well up and lump in his throat like to three-hour-old gravy.

He wants the words for a reply to the preacher. He wants the words out of respect for his mother.

They never come.

They cannot come.

Without the words, he falls into the arms of the mountain preacher and cries just like the day his mother brought him into the world on that very same bed where she now lay corpse.

At the conclusion of the funeral, Jim Bob thanks the preacher for a moving, respectful, and gracious eulogy and service. He strolls to the car and finds the supporting and loving arms of his family. Holding the passenger car door ajar for his wife as she buckles her seat belt, he leans in and whispers gently, *Guess who is comin' to dinner tomorrow night?*

She responds in kind, *Who?*

He winks and smiles, answering, *It's a seepuckerin' preaches who says Jesus loves me!*

One just never knows.

One just never knows how God works in our lives and through whom God chooses.

The Smoky Mountain Version of the Book of Ruth is a story about the movement of God in our world, in ways least expected.

Yes, another Smoky Mountain Version of God's good news—hillbilly style.

KNOXVILLE GIRL

The Making of a President

A Smoky Mountain Version (SMV)

Adapted from and based on the Book of Ruth

(Ruth 1:1-22)

TURN AWAY, TURN BACK

South Bound on I-65

There is a man by the name of Leroy.

He lives with his family in the community of "Sunbeam," also known as "The Land of Bread," just outside Chicago. Times are hard and "bread" is scarce.

One day, however, they leave, heading southeast in search of a different kind of bread.

Leroy goes to live and work as a park ranger in the mountain town of Townsend, Tennessee, nestled in the southwestern shadows of the Great Smoky Mountains.

Leroy takes his wife, Elizabeth, and two sons with him. Elizabeth's family and closest friends have nicknamed her, "Sweetness." No matter her conversational partner, Elizabeth always finishes her "good-byes" with a blessing of sorts, *You be sweet!*

Nicknames.

Family and friends do those kinds of things—give nicknames.

Leroy and Sweetness have two sons.

"Chigger."

"Skeleton."

They all go to Townsend, southbound on I-65, and take up living there.

Shortly thereafter, Leroy dies from an accidental hanging, or so the locals say.

Coworkers report that as he climbs a tree to inspect the nest of a rare species of bird, Leroy loses his balance and falls towards the ground.

During the fall, unfortunately, the "safety" rope wraps around Leroy's neck and before anyone can cut him loose, he strangles to death.

"A lynching without guilty hands, observes a devastated onlooker.

Elizabeth is a widower now, with two younguns.

Those boys grow into men and both take "southern" women as wives.

Chigger takes Leena as his wife.

Skeleton marries Jenny Sue, aka, Knoxville Girl.

Leena looks very much like Elizabeth. Sharing similar bone structure, facial features, hair textures and color, both can pass as models for *Ebony* magazine. They look mighty fine when they is dressed to the "tee!"

And Lord have mercy! They both have the darkest brown eyes—glistening and enchanting dollops of the richest and finest chocolate!

Now, Jenny Sue she is different.

Real different.

Jenny Sue's eyes are as green as cat eyes.

Her skin is as milky white as biscuit flour.

And she is never without her short, striped polyester miniskirt and halter top.

Lord have mercy, her hair stands as tall and proud as Stonewall Jackson. She denies that it takes a whole can of Aqua Net to hold it in place.

Skeleton's family does not understand or appreciate his attraction to Jenny Sue. At best, they tolerate it; yet they honor his choice. Family needs to stick together, you know.

The family does just that. They stick together like Jenny Sue's hairdo, until ten years later.

Chigger dies in a fistfight with "Calamine."

'Nuff said.

Skeleton loses his life by a different hand of fate.

Skeleton loves playing cards, loves playing for "bread." His nickname is "No-Guts" because of his timid card play during high-stake situations.

One night, however, someone goes too far with the name-calling.

You got no guts, Skeleton! You think long, you think wrong! Show some guts and call my hand! You got no guts!

Between the courage mustered by too much "white lightning" and pride, Skeleton loses his temper.

He returns the taunt by calling the player a "cheat."

Cheat!

In defense of his name and honor, the poker-playing partner pulls a knife, a big one at that.

He uses it only after Skeleton pulls a gun from his back pocket and threatens to shoot his skinny "arse." There is no shot. The knife is quicker, this time.

Skeleton dies right there with a "full house" in his hand.

Elizabeth now has lost her husband and both sons.

Elizabeth is empty-handed.

For Elizabeth, life becomes hard and bitter. It no longer has a sweet taste.

I should have never come to this husband-and-son-forsaken and no bread of a mountain in the first place, she laments.

Elizabeth receives word from back home in Chicago that the economy is doing better than ever since the election of a new president.

Her auntie says, *God is just a'blessin' us with everythin'. Why don't you just come on back home, girl?*

Elizabeth accepts. *It wouldn't be right to miss out on God's blessin's,* she says to herself.

Westbound on I-40

No!

Elizabeth rebukes her two daughters-in-law who want to go to Chicago with her.

No, you ain't goin' with me. Y'all git back to your folks.

It surprises her how much she sounds like her daughters-in-law.

Go back each one of ya. Git back to your mama's house. May Jesus deal kindly with ya. He ain't been so good to me of late. I hope for nothin' but the best for you younguns. Maybe you can even find a husband someday. I know your mamas are worried about ya both. Y'all git on back and go home, and you be sweet!

Her *"you be sweet!"* is difficult to utter, though.

Life for Elizabeth is far too bitter.

She kisses, hugs, and squeezes them both.

They all cry just like the days when Leroy, Chigger, and Skeleton died.

Despite Elizabeth's pleas, Leena and Jenny Sue will not have any more of this "leavin'" stuff. They reply in unison and as though they have rehearsed it. *Nope, we ain't goin'! We are a'goin' north with ya!*

Now listen here! Elizabeth demands. *Why in the Sam Hill would you want to go with me? I haven't been with a man since Leroy died. I ain't going to have any more babies. And I don't think I'm the*

Sarah or the Mary type, either. I don't see any younguns coming from me for you to marry. Don't look to me for any assurance of walkin' down the aisle again. So, y'a'll go back home and git on with your lives. You have been like daughters to me, but this life has put a bitter taste in my mouth right now! So Y'ALL leave and YOU be sweet!

They cry, again.

Arm in arm, crying.

Leena, always the one to do as told, kisses her mother-in-law on her cheek for the last time and leaves, heading back home to Alabama.

She lets go and departs because Elizabeth asks her, not because she wants to leave.

Be sweet, Mama, Leena whispers in the ear of Elizabeth.

Jenny Sue remains, defiantly.

Elizabeth, held in the rebellious clutch of Jenny Sue, says, *Now, young lady, it's your turn to go. Be a good girl and do what Leena has done. See...she's a'walkin'. You need to do the same. You head on back to Knoxville, girl!*

Jenny Sue replies, *I ain't goin.' I've seen far more goin's than I have seen comin's. There ain't no way I'm goin' to leave you like my daddy left us when I was a baby youngun.*

Elizabeth thinks about responding, *I ain't your daddy!* but doesn't.

Jenny Sue continues, *Wherever you be, I be.*

Elizabeth wants to say, *Yeah right! Now where did I put my NASCAR tickets?* She bites her tongue instead.

Jenny Sue is not finished. *Where you sleep, I'll sleep.*

Elizabeth almost declares but thinks better, *You won't catch me in no trailer home!*

And your folks will be my folks and your Jesus will surely be my Jesus, Jenny Sue offers sincerely.

Now that's about as far as this can go, Elizabeth mumbles, but not loud enough for Jenny Sue to hear.

Not able to hold back, Elizabeth barks in response. *We might be able to go to the same places, do the same things, and maybe sleep in the same places, but Chicago ain't ready for some old tired-lookin' Grandma Moses and a Dolly Parton-lookin' wanna-be!*

She loves Jenny Sue with all her heart, so don't get the wrong idea about Elizabeth.

Don't be hard on her.

However, one can handle only so much mayonnaise on their pinto beans! Jenny Sue is dolloping on too much for Elizabeth's taste for the time being.

Jenny Sue has yet to finish, though.

I'll be with you till your dyin' day or my dyin' day, which ever comes first. All I want is to be buried beside ya, so that I'll never leave ya like my daddy did one too many times, she cries.

Jenny Sue's love and loyalty moves and touches Elizabeth. She cannot think of anything in response to Jenny Sue. Her heart is feeling a love that words can't express. A tugging not overcome with mere words.

Finally, Jenny Sue concludes, *And as Jesus as my witness, let it be so!*

When Elizabeth sees that Jenny Sue is determined to go with her, she relents.

They both leave for Sunbeam, westbound on I-40.

(Ruth 2:1-23)

TURNING TO EACH OTHER

Back at Wonderland

Elizabeth returns to Sunbeam with Jenny Sue in tow. When Elizabeth and Jenny Sue arrive in Sunbeam, the whole community comes out, as it is rumored that Dolly Parton is a' comin' that way.

It is rather a funny sight.

Can you imagine? An old tired Grandma Moses followed by a Dolly Parton wanna-be in Chicago of all places?

Some of the women standing in the crowd of that two-person parade inquire among themselves, *Is that Elizabeth? Is that our Miss Lizzy? Is that our Sweetness?*

Elizabeth barks to them. *There ain't no more sugar in this canister! Call me an angry black woman if you wish because Jesus done gone and made me mad! I left this place with a good husband and two darlin' childr'n. And now I ain't got a pot to pee in!*

Why me?

Why, God?

Why me?

And don't ya dare call me "Sweetness!

Though no one knows Jenny Sue, everyone knows her kind.

Some call her "whitey."

Others call her "trash."

Many just call her "white trash."

Someone among the crowd declares, *Skeleton done gone and got his family some of that southern white sugar cane. Now why would he have gone done that? Don't he knowed that too much sugar is harmful to one's health? It will just kill a man!"*

They return to Sunbeam just in time!

Maybe.

Jenny Sue Gets Busy

By Leroy's side of the family, Elizabeth has kin who have done well amidst God's blessings.

Richard is his name.

The recent economic boom has made a turn for the better for him and the rest of the town.

Jenny Sue, knowing how Elizabeth is a' feeling down about things, offers to go and find some work to make ends meet.

Jenny Sue jokingly says that she is tired of having to put her foot in her mouth just to make the "ends" meet.

Elizabeth does not appreciate the humor, and expresses none.

Bitterness can make one feel so dark that it's like crawling around the insides of a cow, Jenny Sue wants to say to Elizabeth, but doesn't.

She does say to her, however, *I have just got to get some work! I'll see if I can find some and see if I can make a friend or two in this place. They ain't too friendly around here. Do you like my outfit?*

Elizabeth's only response is, *Go on 'then!*

So she goes.

Jenny Sue goes to the nearest factory and finds work rather quickly.

Now, mind ya, she doesn't start with the best of jobs. She takes the offering of a job—cleaning bathrooms, mopping, dusting, and such around the plant.

Work is work, she says proudly.

She does not know, however, that the factory belongs to Richard.

Richard returns that morning from a delivery. As always, he greets the workers as he makes his way through the plant and to his office.

Mornin'! he says, and the replies seldom stray from one in kind, *Mornin'!, Dick!*

Once in his office, Richard inquires of a supervisor. *Who is that white woman? And who in the world dresses her? Did you get a look at her? Looks like a Goodwill special to me!*

The supervisor replies. *She is that white trash that came in with Elizabeth. I've never seen so much hair spray in one place than I have seen in that beehive of a do! And listen to the way that chicken clucks. She surely is southern fried! Anyway, she came here and said, "Please, let me work. I'll be glad just to pick up after everyone else." You know that we've been needin' some janitorial help. Now she doesn't have any fashion taste but I'll be doggone if she ain't a right good worker though. She has been out there since the crack of dawn. Why, good lard, she hadn't even taken time to pee. She just keeps a' workin'.*

Happy as a Cat with Rat Breath

Richard, later in the day, instructs Jenny Sue. *Now listen, and you pay me mind. Never you pay any attention to the foolishness a few of these guys might start. Some of these jokers might just want to start givin' you a hard time. I've told my supervisor that if anybody starts anythin' with you, they will answer directly to me. If they start somethin', then their tails are grass and I'm the lawn mower. Now, when you get thirsty or hungry, the supervisor will make sure that you get somethin'. Okay?*

Such kindheartedness moves Jenny Sue. It is the first kind word by someone since a'comin' to Sunbeam.

So moved by the gesture, she buries her face in her hands and begins to sob, quietly.

Somewhat embarrassed by her public demonstration, she seeks more control and inquires of Richard in between her sobs. *Why are you treatin' me so kindly? Why are you so nice to me? I know that I am the only "snowball" out here, so why? Why are you being so kind? You know that I ain't from these parts, don't ya?*

"The dickens you say," replies a half smiling Richard. *I know more about you than you ever dreamed. Hear you from Knoxville, girl. And all that you have done for Elizabeth is the talk of the town. You got some nerve, though. You a'comin' to this place.*

You know that you are the only white woman within a country mile, don't you? Mighty nice of you, though, to stick with Miss Lizzy the way you gone and done.

Surely, Jesus will take notice of what you have done for that old widow woman. I'm sure of that. Yep! Jesus done wrote it down and put it in his book. "Knoxville Girl, the whitest white woman in all the world done and taken up house with a bunch of black folk."

Yep, done wrote that down. And since Jesus done wrote it, that's good enough for me. In this world, Jesus don't put up with foolishness. And since Jesus don't put up with it, I don't either. You'll be safe and sound here. I guarantee it. Why, before you know it, you will be as happy as a cat with rat breath.

Richard hesitantly but lovingly puts his arms around her, reassuring.

You just don't know how your kind words have made me feel. You're so sweet. Jenny Sue whispers amidst the awkward embrace.

When it comes lunchtime, Richard invites Jenny Sue to eat, saying, *Come here and get you some fried catfish and hush puppies.*

Richard saves a spot for her at the wooden picnic table that serves as the dining area in the middle of the plant.

She eats the fish and puppies with Richard and the rest of the work crew.

It has been awhile since she ate like this. Soon she is filling as full as a summer tick on a hound dog. They give her some leftovers for an afternoon snack, tucked away in a white grocers' bag.

Upon returning to work, Richard instructs the supervisor. *Let her work as much as she wants to work. She could use the overtime pay.*

She works until late.

Richard makes sure she receives her pay that same evening.

After work, Jenny Sue returns to Elizabeth and tells her how generous and gracious the factory owner has been to her.

He never told me his name. I didn't ask. But he sure was good to me…and here…you want some fried catfish and hush puppies? she inquires as she hands Elizabeth the white greasy bag that contains the gift given earlier.

Elizabeth is curious about who would have been so kind, *Where did you work? May Jesus be sweet to the man who did all that!*

Jenny Sue describes the place where she worked that day, as well as doing her best to depict the physical features of the factory owner.

Why, good lard, landlard, that's Dick! Well, his real name is Richard. The good Lard don't forget the living or the dead! Dat man is Leroy's kin. I remember that Leroy thought Richard hanged the moon and polished the stars. But you've got to be careful out there. Now, Jenny Sue, you shame the devil and tell the full truth. Did any of those men bother you at the plant?

Jenny Sue replies, *Now, Mama, you knowed that I can't look this good without turnin' a head or two. No! No one bothered me. Richard made sure of that.*

(Ruth 3:1-18)

TURNING TO A STRANGER

Night Crawlers are Good for Fishing

After a couple of years, Elizabeth says to Jenny Sue, *My darling, you have been the daughter to me that I have never had or ever will. So don't take what I am about to say in the wrong way.*

You need to think about the future. You can't spend the rest of your life in the factory.

So it is time to do a little night fishin'.

Richard will be workin' late at the office. He usually eats his meals there, as I hear. He has no one at home anymore.

You go to the factory tonight and wait till he goes to bed. He often sleeps there. He'll be a little heavy with malt, so go and lay down with him and from there he just might tell ya what he needs or wants. Maybe, just maybe, your wants are his needs. Maybe his wants are your needs.

Jenny Sue replies, *Do you think that I'm nothin' more than white trash?*

There is no reply.

But I hear what you are saying," Jenny Sue continues. *Now where's my pink vest and my cooler for the night crawlers?*

Jenny Sue goes that night to Richard's office and does as Elizabeth instructs.

Jenny Sue watches the shadow of Richard through the small window on the east side of the office with the aid of the full harvest moon.

The shadowy figure of Richard makes its way to the cluttered cot in the corner of the room.

Richard lies down.

After an hour or so, Jenny Sue quietly makes her way through the unlocked door and carefully folds her petite frame into the form created by the slumbering body of Richard.

Up to this point, everything unfolds just as Elizabeth said it would.

Late in the night and early in the morning, the malt begins to knock on the door of Richard's bladder. As he stirs, he is startled to find a woman curled and molded to his body.

And a white woman at that!

At first, he thinks it is a dream. He's been having a lot of dreams about a lot of women lately. Loneliness creates its own reality.

I must be drunk, he says to himself when he realizes that he is not dreaming.

But how did this happen? he asks himself as he gestures towards the sleeping woman at his side, and manages to utter. *What the...Who the...Who in the name of Dolly Parton?*

Startled from her slumber, Jenny Sue awakes rubbing her eyes and replies, *Well, I'm Jenny Sue, Knoxville Girl, you know. Are you lonely?*

Yes, well! Thank you, Jesus! No! No! I mean, what?

Richard's stammering tongue can hardly keep pace with his racing heart.

I've never been with a white...Oh wow...I mean...let's slow this down a bit. I know that things are hard for you and Miss Lizzy but I'm not interested in buyin' anythang.

I'm not selling anything! she declares.

But surely there are other men...men who are more like you... you know what I mean...Now don't get me wrong, Richard begs, confessing. *I'm deeply flattered. You can have any of the young men you want and here you show up at my office in the middle of the night and in the middle of my bed! But we are kin, at least by marriage, but that's a long way back. But you stay here tonight and we'll sort through all this stuff out in the mornin'. You can lay back down. I need to find the bathroom.*

She stays all night but gets up and leaves early in the morning before anyone can see her there.

In their night conversation, Richard insists that it just wouldn't look good or decent for anyone to see her here under these circumstances.

There's a reason they call night fishin', night fishin', he chuckles.

Before she leaves, however, Richard puts some money in her vest pocket.

I didn't sell anything! she replies somewhat angrily as she discovers the money.

I didn't buy anything! he retorts.

Upon returning home, Elizabeth inquires, *How did thangs go? Are you all right?*

Jenny Sue tells her everything.

In the midst of the conversation Jenny Sue reaches into her vest pocket and pulls out the roll of money that Richard has given her, saying, *He said to take this to Miss Lizzy...I know that thangs are difficult.*

Mum, Elizabeth replies as she strokes her chin in reflection. *I wonder what he meant by that sorting through the other stuff? Thoughtful of him, ain't it? I'm talkin' about the money, dear.*

There's Just Something About Jenny Sue

Later that morning, Richard finds his best friend and tells of the night's surprise.

So, inquires Richard to his buddy, *What do you think?*

What do I think? the friend replies with ire. *First of all, are you insane? I can see you before the judge now. When he axes, "How do you plead to the charge of datin' a white woman?" you can say, 'I plead insanity, sir." Now, imagine what might happen to you if someone comes to your place and finds you with that white woman.*

You must have been worried about that by askin' her to leave so early. Besides, from what I'm hearin', she's a sort on the trashy side.

Now you know exactly what I mean. Sounds like she came in the night to make trouble. White trashy women are like that. Now you knowed that be the truth! I wouldn't trust her. So, reel it in, Dick. But what's this about you carin' for this here woman?

Well, Richard confesses, *she just seems so lovable, sincere, honest, and loyal and she's downright smart. My heart races when I'm around her, her green eyes. I'm hooked. The way she walks and talks just overtakes me like a fragrance that leaps out from a newly opened bottle of expensive perfume.*

And, good lard, look how she has stuck with Miss Lizzy! There is just somethin' about Jenny Sue. Maybe I'm not too far removed from the South to like my women a little on the trashy side, he concludes with a nervous chuckle.

Hold on, Bubba!" retorts his friend.

Lets stop this train before it goes through of the tunnel at Missionary Ridge. You're a'tellin' me that you got the hots for this white woman and there is nothing I can say to cool you off?

I guess.

You guess? Now tell me, what's the next thing you are going to do, marry her?

Gave it some thought.

Now, you must be out of your ever lovin' mind! Not only will you catch it from the white folks, you are sure goin' to catch it from our folks.

A white woman? Indeed!

Our folks and the white folks will line up to greet you. You know how generous we all can be! On that day, we'll be passing out lollipops and butt-kickin's. And by the time we get to you, we'll be out of lollipops! And I'll be the first in line!

Now I'm saying all this because I'm your friend. I want you... No! I need you to hear it from me straight. I would never think about marryin' a white woman. If you ever hear of me doing such a stupid thang as that, you'll know that my cheese has done gone and slid off my cracker.

"Well, I get the point," replies Richard. *No need to belabor it.*

Shame the devil, and tell the truth," the friend inquires. *"Do you love her?*

Yes, I do...I do love her..." Richard confidently sighs.

Well, I guess your insanity plea with hold. Sounds like you are crazy about her!

(Ruth 4:1-22)

THE STRANGE TURN

The Genealogy of a President

Richard proposes and takes Jenny Sue as his marriage partner for life. And before they knowed it, Jesus has gone and blessed them with the prettiest baby this side of the Mississippi.

It is hard to tell who is more proud about that youngun, though.

Richard and Jenny Sue both have that "mama crow look." Everyone knows that a mama crow thinks its baby is the blackest.

The beaming pride of Miss Lizzy is the talk of the town, however, for one of her many prayers has come to be!

Just as the sun beams through the morning mist on a fall mountain day, that youngun just lights up the life of that proud woman!

Everywhere Miss Lizzy goes, she has that baby in tow, cuddling and snuggling him in her warm and reassuring bosom.

The community folk give that baby a nickname.

Nicknames are important.

Nicknames are a family's claim and a community's embrace.

They nickname him, *Governor!* Or *Gov,* for short.

That child done took over this whole state, some of the folk jokingly say.

Who could have ever guessed?

Who would have ever imagined that "Governor" was to be the granddaddy of the first African-American president of these United States?

Now, this president would be famous for more than just being the first black chief executive.

The country would hail and applaud this president, not just for compassionate and fair executive leadership.

This president will save the country.

There will be no invading army for this sitting president to reveal such a distinguished character of valor.

No army.

No invasion.

What will distinguish this president will be the ability to make the country respect folk solely by the content of their character and nothing more.

Yes, this president will save the country from itself!

Yes, this president is the grandchild of ole "Governor," whose mama is Jenny Sue, aka Knoxville Girl.

Imagine that!

This president often reflects on these roots from the mountains.

In addition, I'm here to say, she is darn proud!

Yes, the president is done proud of her mountain pedigree!

THE LAST WORDS

A Biblical Interpretation and Mapping of the Book of Ruth: My Road to *Knoxville Girl*

How did *Knoxville Girl* come into being?

The answer lies in a small book of the Hebrew Scriptures about a rather obscure Moabite woman.

Through the peripheral world of ancient Israel and in a literary character by the name of Ruth, I find familiar voices, similar cultural patterns, and landscapes akin to my southern Appalachian roots.

Between the ancient worlds of Israel and Moab, I discover "kin" that I did not know I had.

The influences of my Appalachian roots and my place within the spectrum of the dominant American culture define my ancestry as "hillbilly."

The hillbilly and the Moabite in the character of Ruth seem to have a lot in common.

Apart from telling the story of a hillbilly girl who is the great grandmother of the first African-American President, *Knoxville Girl* is about God's redemption and the reversal of the assumptions that originally intended to demean and oppress.

Based upon a suggested interpretative model by Fredrick C. Tiffany and Sharon H. Ringe, *Knoxville Girl* emerges out of a method that is "relational" in its assumption and "interactive" in its method.[2]

As opposed to the notion that one extracts "truth" from a superfluous sheathing, the Tiffany/Ringe model assumes that "truth" of scripture emerges from the intersection of reader and text.

In other words, truth is not something that is "mined, uncovered, or shelled." Rather, truth emerges out of a relationship. *Meaning thus occurs not in isolated words or signs, but in the relationships of those words within and between the worlds....* [3]

As I explore the Book of Ruth, "truth" is not just limited to biblical analysis and critical assessment but also emerges from the text of both Ruth's world and my world with roots in southern Appalachia.

It is not enough just to "know" the world of Ruth or simply to know the facts of my own world. Biblical interpretation mapping requires interchange, *Since meaning occurs in the interaction between the text and those who receive it, and is not defined or delimited by the text alone, each new occasion with a text will create new meanings.* [4]

Since "truth" exists "relationally" and through the "interaction" of worlds, what is the method for interpretation?

Tiffany/Ringe offer five "stages" or "steps" to map out a plausible interpretation that respects the integrity of the Scriptures and demands the reader's participation. Karl Barth suggests that God's Word *demands...more than notice, or understanding, or sympathy. It demands participation, comprehension, co-operation; for it is a communication which presumes faith in the living God, and which creates that which it presumes.* [5]

These stages are fivefold: (1) "starting at home," (2) "encountering the text," (3) "close reading," (4) "reading contextually," and finally (5) "engaging the text."[6]

For reasons I state later, my mapping starts at "encountering the text." After reversing these first two stages, I follow their model thereafter.

This is the method of my interpretive mapping of the Book of Ruth. It serves to answer "how" *Knoxville Girl* came to be.

The Book of Ruth

The Book of Ruth is only four chapters in length, so it reads quickly. I began my mapping with the "New Revised Standard Version," followed by using the translation from "The New International Version."

The "Ruth" of Eugene Peterson's *The Message* keeps before me the notion of narrative and story.

Encountering the Text

I must start with God's story before I start with my own story. As the noted theologian and scholar Walter Bruggeman suggests, God's story is *so powerful and compelling, so passionate and uncompromising in its anguish and hope that it requires that we submit our experience to it and thereby reenter our experience on new terms, namely the terms of the text.* [7]

Therefore, I begin with the text, the story of Ruth.

As I read, I note my first "impressions."[8]

What catches my attention?

What slows down my reading?

What "speed bumps" encourage a closer look and deeper investigation at the landscape of the text?[9]

In my initial reading of the text of Ruth, a few things "slowed" me down.

First, what is the significance of the names? Is there a message in the names alone?

Elimelech, Bethlehem, Naomi, Orpah, Mahlon, Chilion, Boaz, and Moab. Who are they and what do the names mean?

My appreciation, however and for whatever reason, goes out to Ruth. Her loyalty and cunning ways intrigue me.

And what about the "sexuality" within the story?

Naomi appears to "know the ropes" and the "power of sex." She tutors Ruth in its "powerfulness," or so it seems?

What of Naomi's instructions to Ruth?

Is it possible for Naomi to be a heroine?

Is Ruth a heroine as well?

On the other hand, is Ruth's "claim to fame" assured only as a mother, a mother of an important male?

Is Boaz a "typical male" who takes advantage of the situation? Does he portray the old adage that "women need a reason for sex, men only need a place?" Whereas I admit, that one assumption is inaccurate and the other deplorable, yet are they part of the storyline?

I am "overwhelmed" by the "vulnerability" that Ruth, Naomi, and Oprah experience.

Given this vulnerability, I am "gripped" completely by Naomi's public declaration of being "bitter." I would call it being "pissed off."

There is a line in a movie that stars Jack Nicholson, Helen Hunt and Greg Kinnear, entitled, *As Good as It Gets.*

Nicholson's character, who lives sometimes responsibly but most times irresponsibly with an obsessive, compulsive disorder, offers to drive a man, who is gay, to his parents' home out of state. The young gay man, portrayed by Greg Kinnear, though seeking financial assistance, really seeks some reconciliation with them. However, he cannot drive himself to his family because he is recovering from a mugging and a severe beating, which is cause for his financial crisis. Nicholson offers to drive only because of a love "interest" with Hunt's character, who is making the trip as well.

As the gay man laments his past, the separation from his family, and his present state in general, Nicholson sternly scolds in reply. *You are not pissed off because you have it so bad. You're pissed because others have it so good!* I think of that declaration when I read Naomi's "name change" to "Mara." I know what it means to have, harbor, and possess "bitterness."

Finally, what is important about the Book of Ruth? Canonically, it seems "squeezed" between Judges and Samuel.

What is that all about?

Starting at Home

The journey of interpretation begins at *home, with attention to the immediate contemporary environment in which the biblical text is encountered.* [10]

The journey begins with an honest inventory of my being and my world.

I begin by asking, "Who am I? To whom do I belong?"

I am a white male of southern Appalachian ancestry, hillbilly roots.

Often times, my greatest fear is that I will get beyond my raising.

At other times, I must!

I am the oldest of five children.

Dad, can I ask you some questions?

As a junior in high school, my English class was given an assignment to write a short biography of any notable or known person. I chose my father as the subject.

Dad, can I ask you some questions?

Sure. What kind?

Well I'm doing a project for English class and I want to write about you.

Me?

Sure, why not?

But why?

That's easy, I replied. *Cause you are my dad.*

Thinking upon our exchange, I initially took his "Why?" as an indication of some reservation. Maybe he didn't think he was worthy of such melodrama. On the other hand, maybe he was simply "taken back" a bit, i.e., shocked that I had even taken the time to ask, to ask about him, his family, my family.

It was probably the latter.

At that time, I didn't know much about my dad except for some "immediate" facts.

He met mom at a bus station in Knoxville, Tennesscе.

My mom was there to "send off" a brother to the military. My dad was there, alone I think, heading to military service as well. I don't know what sparked their conversation. I need to ask.

They later married in 1954.

I was born in 1956.

My father had recently retired from the Air Force at the time of my writing assignment.

Since that retirement, we had relocated to Four Way Inn, a small semi-rural community outside of Knoxville, Tennessee, where my mother had relatives.

Dad was born and raised in Townsend, Tennessee, a small community located in the western foothills of southern Appalachia. The town lost its timber industry with the establishment of the national park known as the Great Smoky Mountains. Now it claims to be the "Peaceful Side" of the mountains.

Dad enjoyed sports.

He was a mechanic.

He snored, loudly.

One of his favorite breakfast dishes included scrambled eggs smothered with pig brains.

These are just a few of the "facts" that I knew about my father at the time.

I had never asked about "how and from whom he came."

I knew "Grandma," his mother.

She lived in Cincinnati, Ohio. We saw her about every five years or so. She loved Burtons snuff and the Cincinnati Reds. I never knew the man my father might have called "Father."

I began my interview with a proper, formal, and professional interrogation technique: *Just the facts, Dad. Just the facts!*

I learned some new things about my father.

He played a year of college football.

While a senior in high school, he asked his English teacher out for a date.

I replied that was out of the question for me. *I would not want to been seen dead with my English teacher!*

Dad left home at the age of fifteen because of an abusive and negligent father who spent time in the state penitentiary for bigamy.

He supported his mother and siblings with after-school work.

I soon discovered, to my amazement, that my father's telling was far more than "just the facts." His family story began to unfold. Stories of pain, fear, abandonment, and celebrations were revisited, relived, and revealed.

In short, I knew some rather basic information, facts if you will, about my father.

However, I did not know his story—in turn, my story as well—until then.

My story, furthermore, took on greater significance and meaning when I became involved in a small United Methodist congregation, Pleasant Hill United Methodist Church, which is tucked away among some gently rolling hills of east Tennessee.

Though raised in a loving and secure home, as I overheard church folk talking about roots in a larger family, God's family, I felt a little like Dick Gregory sitting on the back porch. I did not feel "rooted" or "connected" to a people:

> *...it bugged me when the other kids in the neighborhood were called in to eat dinner. We'd be playing, and all of sudden they'd have to leave to eat. I'd just wait on their back porches until they were through eating and ready to come out to play again. It's a funny feeling to be by your self on a back porch and hear people eating, people talking. There's no talk in the world like the warm, happy talk of a family at the dinner table....* [11]

It seems rather strange but true, though. I never seriously inquired nor engaged my family's story, or even my own, until I began hearing the "gospel story." In hearing this story, I heard an invitation to be part of a larger family.

It was in a high school English class assignment that I began to unearth some of my familial roots in folks like Fredrick, Jacob, Daniel, Juliana, William Oliver, Carrie, Stanley Freeman and Willard John, who would later change his name to John Willard.

My discovery was just more than "facts," though.

What began to emerge for my benefit was a story of stories about some German immigrants forging an unknown future.

Beginning with wanderings from a seaport in Philadelphia, Pennsylvania in the late eighteenth century, my ancestors followed the riches and demands of in-laws to the western foothills of southern Appalachia—where whiskey and church were among the most important aspects of community life, i.e., "hillbilly" community life.

It was in the hearing and experiencing the gospel story of Jesus and the experience of love, grace, and acceptance of the risen Jesus through and by a small congregation that my life story also unearthed some far more numerous "familial" roots. Folks like Abraham, Sarah, Hagar, Ishmael, Isaac, Rebekah, Jacob, Esau, Leah, Rachel, Martha, Peter, Mary, and Paul, along with a multitude others, emerge as a family unknown and now gained.

Meaning and a sense of belonging began to dawn.

Only later in life have I discovered that my story makes sense, best sense, if not "only" sense, in the context of God's story.

The intersection between the stories of a people and the story of God are best articulated, expressed, and conveyed through narration, not as a summary or litany of facts.

My father is much more than a collection of facts. The facts of his life are held together by a story of stories.

With my high school English paper completed, I soon discovered that I was beginning a journey of self-discovery initiated and revealed by an experience of the risen Christ and his community.

Close Reading and Reading Contextually

Moving from an "initial" reading, I attempt a more in-depth exploration of the story of Ruth.

Each word of the text needs engaging, from the first to the last. Attention to vocabulary, grammar, logic, etc., are all important entrees into the text.[12]

Matthew's gospel names Ruth within the genealogy of Jesus.[13] So the Book of Ruth is not only important to ancient Israel, it (and she) is important to the early church. How is Ruth important to each?

Ruth, within the Jewish canonical order, finds her place there for liturgical reasons.[14]

The public reading of Ruth occurs during the festival of "Weeks," which marks the end of the barley season and the beginning of the wheat season. Part of the *Five Scrolls,* Ruth becomes "associated" with the season of harvest, the late spring of the year.

Ruth's place within the liturgical year also coincides with the remembrance of God giving the Torah on Mount Sinai. Within this scheme, tradition celebrates Ruth as a convert to Judaism, and Boaz is the ultimate law keeper and righteous man.

Within the Christian canon, the Book of Ruth serves as a "chronological" placement. Placed between the books of Judges and Samuel, it serves to bridge the period of ancient governance from the "rule of judges" to the "rule of a king." The early church saw the Book of Ruth as further proof that God is still active in the affairs of the world.

Most scholars place the authorship of Ruth between 950 and 700 BCE.[15] The Book of Ruth is more than a mere "historical" record of the time period.

It is a story among stories.

A God story at that!

Based on a literary perspective, however, the book of Ruth just might be an *artistically constructed, kaleidoscopic narrative that is more like an extended parable than a historical record.* [16]

It is this perspective of Ruth as *parable* that I find most helpful.

What is the *parable* of Ruth?

What is the message?

What is the new insight or paradigm?

The paradigm is rather simple: "Reversal is the essence of redemption."[17] In a book that contains only eighty-five verses, the word for "redeem" (and its derivatives, e.g., redeemer, redemption) is used twenty-three times.[18] But God's activity, at least from the perspective of the people's history, must be experiential. From whence does God's activity emerge, or take place? The answer, according to Ruth, "lies," no pun intended, in a world of reversal, in the world of God's reversal. New life opportunities emerge and start from the "margins" of life as opposed to the "centers of power." It moves from "pie-in-the-sky" to a more "earthy" location.

Ruth, a Moabite, becomes the instrument of God's redemption for Naomi and Naomi's Israelite people.

The Moabites carry, however, "negative moral and emotional connotations" for ancient Israelites.[19] This point is not subtle or lost in story.

Such cultural "disdain" is codified within the tradition. In Deuteronomy 23:3, Moabites are "forbidden" in the religious assembly of Israel. Part of the Israelite tradition "remembers" that when Israelite men became sexually involved with Moabite women, apostasy follows.[20]

The paradigm of the Book of Ruth becomes much more "visible" within its "tradition."

The formula of the tradition concludes:

Moabites (women) + Israelites (men) = Apostasy.

The Book of Ruth, applying the "essence of reversal," reformulates it this way:

Moabite (Ruth) + Israelite (Boaz) =
Redemption (Naomi/Israel).

What of the names?

Elimelech means "My God is King!" Yet he goes to a foreign land of a foreign god/king?

Bethlehem is a "House of Bread"; there is no bread, however, in the land of bread?

Naomi is "pleasant" but declares her "bitterness."

Ruth will be a "friend or companion" through "thick and thin," and a Moabite at that!

Orpah denotes the "back of the neck." That is what you see when she returns home to her people.

Mahlon just may be "sickness," as unto death.

Chilion signifies "spent" as in "no more," "dead."

Boaz suggests "in him is strength." Is the strength social and/or sexual power? Or religious righteousness? Or both? Or all three?

Moab, as tradition has it, is the land of the sexual deviant—a pre-modern white trash culture?

The most famous and most quoted lines include Ruth's pledge to Naomi:

"'Do not press me to leave you or to turn back from following you!

Where you go, I will go;
where you lodge, I will lodge;
your people shall be my people,
and your God my God.
Where you die, I will die—
there will I be buried.
May the LORD do thus and so to me,
and more as well,
if even death parts me from you!'"[21]

However, Naomi never responds. The Midrash offers Naomi's voice to Ruth's pledge. It is a powerful, insightful and stirring option:

> *The sages say that Ruth's speech to Naomi reflected a conversation and that certain parts of it were offered in answer to specific statements by Naomi. Naomi's part of the conversation unfortunately was not included in the Scripture text. For example, when Ruth said she would go with Naomi, her mother-in-law responded that Jewish women did not go to theaters and circuses. To this Ruth responded that she would simply follow Naomi's example, "Wherever you go I will go." Then Naomi told her that she could not live in a house that did not have mezuzah on the door. Ruth replied, "Wherever you live I will live." When Ruth said, "Your people will be my people," she was saying "I will leave all idolatry behind." And with, "Your God will be my God," Ruth expressed her dependence on the God of Israel alone.* [22]

This imagined conversation finds a place in *Knoxville Girl.*

Engaging the Text

My interpretation and mapping of Ruth concludes by contrasting the world of Ruth with my world.[23]

"Race" seems to set the tone, pace, and character of the South. Of course, it can be said of the North as well. All too often, our culture divides along the lines of "race."

The first time I read James Cone's *God of the Oppressed*, I said, "Amen! Though a theological treatise on "black theology," it spoke to and for me as a white hillbilly.

Imagine that!

My "amen" did not come out of "liberal white guilt," but because Cone speaks of similar cultural experiences: a mocked ancestry, trivialized and dismissed.

It was like discovering kin that have always lived next door and I just did not know it. As Jim Goad, a rather crude yet direct social commentator, suggests about race in America, *For economic reasons, the trash—be it black, brown, or white—have always lived side by side in America. It's the Gold Card Whites who've always paid to segregate themselves...*[24]

I value his directness in that he is addressing the issue of "classism," which gets lost in contemporary discussions about "race." Through the lens of liberation theology, I conclude that Goad is speaking with "God's preferential option for the poor," i.e., the classless. Though Goad is a skeptic of religion and its institutional incarnations, he seems to be speaking of the same "trashing" phenomenon that Cone's God has the power to overcome, liberate, and redeem.

The Book of Ruth speaks of a God who not only redeems "trash" but who can use "trash" to redeem the rest of the world. That's good news for a hillbilly that is *pissed because there are so many who are well-off while there are so many who have it so bad!*

This is why I wrote *Knoxville Girl.*

I hope that it takes both "seriously" and "playfully" the *parable* that "reversal is the essence of redemption," as suggested in the Book of Ruth.

The character of Jenny Sue carries the heavy baggage of extreme hope. Is it possible that white trash will just be *one place multiculturalism might look for a white identity which does not view itself as the norm from which all other races and ethnicities divide?* [25]

Is such a perspective possible?

Is such a hope a probability?

With God, all things are possible.

With God and if God chooses, God can grow apples on a barbwire fence!

Knoxville Girl raises the possibility that "white trash" can be a "corrective" to the assumption that "whiteness must always equal terror and racism."[26]

Just as in the scripture text, names in the SMV of Ruth take on significance.

Elimelech becomes *Leroy*, who is an African-American who leaves Chicago for Townsend, Tennessee.

Bethlehem is a place of bread. *Sunbeam* is the name of a major bread producer.

Naomi is *Elizabeth*, aka "Sweetness."

Ruth takes on the good southern name *Jenny Sue,* the best friend one could ever want—southern white trash.

Orpah is *Leena,* the only thing a "good girl" exposes is the back of her neck.

Mahlon is renamed *Chigger,* whose only enemy is calamine lotion.

Chilion is known as *Skeleton* because, as the name suggests, is there anything there?

Boaz is *Richard*, aka "Dick."

Moab—the *"South"*—'nuff said.

Conclusion

At best, the SMV of Ruth is an embellishment. It, however, is much more.

I have always found "narrative" a tremendous advantage in preaching and teaching in parish ministry. In good preaching, there is always an invitation to be an "active" participant, not just a "passive" recipient. The Tiffany/Ringe model of biblical interpretation propels me to be intentional about "staying with" the point of intersection between the text and my world. It compels me to be faithful to both God's story and God's people.

One night after writing, I could hardly sleep because I wanted to share the "twist" ending of a female black president.

Would it be an "uh-huh!" moment to another as it was to me?

The theological conclusion of "reversal as the essence of redemption" is the key to my story line and the embellishment of Ruth.

My hope is that it redeems Jenny Sue and her kin. In so doing, it redeems me as well.

In my first draft, I started with a white southern family going north and a widow returning with a black daughter-in-law. However, that story line failed to address the issues raised by Wray and Newitz. My intention is to communicate that "white trash" can be experienced as a counter-testimony to culturally defined and stereotypical "white racist."

The declaration that "whiteness does not always equal terror and racism" could not be addressed with a starting point of a "black" Jenny Sue.

Is there a new day when whiteness (or any other color) is not always terror because others declare it so? While it is one thing for a "white" declaration of "wholeness," I wanted to explore the dynamics of others knowing it to be so as well.

The Christian canon hints at and signals the "parable of reversal."

In the genealogy of Jesus in Matthew's gospel, four women are named among the naming of numerous men. The women mentioned are not "Israelite" or "Jewish," except for Mary. Why is that? Apart from a variety of explanations, the one that moves, inspires, and gives me hope is that the women's presence in the genealogy is a "counter-testimony" to the power politics of life that assume that God endorses what theologian Walter Wink labels, a "selective grading of human beings."[27]

Wink suggests,

{t}he radicalism of Jesus' image of God is hidden by the self-evident picture he draws from nature. God clearly does not favor some with sunshine and others with rain, depending on their righteousness. Yet, society has in every possible way created the impression that only some are in God's favor and the others out. By our dress, color, nationality, wealth, gender, age, education, language, looks, and health, others can recognize instantly where we are blessed or cursed, beloved or rejected... To say that God does not sit atop the pyramid of power legitimating the entire edifice, does not favor some and reject others, is to expose the entire structure as a human contrivance established in defiance of God's very nature. [28]

Knoxville Girl is about defiance, hopefully God's defiance in face of oppression that demeans and enslaves. God always finds a way—a way for new life, resurrected life!

KNOXVILLE GIRL

There is a rather old bluegrass song entitled, "Knoxville Girl." The song is a ballad about a murder in Knoxville.

The lyrics tell of a young man who kills his girlfriend out of "love," a perverted love admittedly.

The chilling words of "Knoxville Girl" are probably a "rewrite of the eighteenth-century Welch ballad, 'Wexford Girl.'"[29]

Here are the lyrics as sung by The Louvin Brothers.

I met a little girl in Knoxville
A town we all know well
And every Sunday evening
In her home I'd dwell
We went to take an evening walk
About a mile from town
I picked a stick up off the ground
And I knocked that fair girl down
She fell down on her bended knees
For mercy she did cry
"Oh Willy, dear, don't kill me yet
I'm unprepared to die"
She never spoke another word
I only beat her more
Until the ground around me
With her blood did flow

I took her by her golden curls
And I dragged her 'round and 'round
Throwing her into the river
That flows from Knoxville town
Go down, go down, you Knoxville girl
With your dark and roving eyes
Go down, go down, you Knoxville girl
You can never be my bride
I started back to Knoxville
Got there about midnight
My mother, she was worried
She woke up in a fright
Saying, "Dear son, what have you done
To bloody up your clothes?"
I told my anxious mother
That I was bleeding in my nose
I called for me a candle
And I called for me a bed
And I called for me a handkerchief
To bind my aching head
I rolled and thrashed the whole night through
All horrors I did see
The devil stood at the foot of my bed
Pointing his finger at me
They carried me down to Knoxville
And put me in a cell
My friends all tried to get me out
But none could grow my bail
I'm here to waste my life away
Down in this dirty old jail
Because I murdered that Knoxville girl
The girl I loved so well.[30]

The death of the young woman haunts me. I rage against the young murderer. I rage even more against the culture that enslaves both.

I want the young man to know more than bitterness. I want him to live in the midst of sweetness, God's grace.

I want the young woman to come out of the watery tomb of the Tennessee River.

I want her to live!

I want more the both of the them.

There are too many overflowing cups in this world, to use the metaphor of Melanie's poem at the beginning. I am grateful for her generosity in sharing her composition. Even more, she articulates what most us feel—an existential angst that avoids and is devoid of simple explanation. Through her imagative and creative gift of verse, Melanie comes rather close of stating the obvious and less than obvious.

I am clinging to the good news of the risen, yet crucified, Jesus, who is the "reversal" of all things and brings about redemption, hope, and life for this world, even for a redneck hillbilly with southern Appalachian roots!

I often reflect on my roots, and I am here to say, I am darn proud of them!

ENDNOTES

[1] *The Oxford Dictionary and Thesaurus: American Edition* (New York: Oxford University Press, 1996), 1080.

[2] See, Frederick C. Tiffany and Sharon H. Ringe. *Biblical Interpretation: A Roadmap* (Nashville: Abingdon Press, 1996).

[3] Ibid, 27.

[4] Tiffany/Ringe, 27.

[5] Karl Barth, *The Epistle to the Romans* , translated from the sixth edition by Edwyn C. Hoskyns (New York: Oxford University Press, 1968), 28.

[6] Ibid.

[7] Walter Bruggeman, ***A Commentary on Jeremiah: Exile and Homecoming***, (Grand Rapids, Michigan: William B. Eerdmans Publishing Company, 1998), 18.

[8] Tiffany and Ringe, 55.

[9] Ibid, 56

[10] Ibid, 25.

[11] Dick Gregory (with Robert Lipsyte). *Nigger* (New York: Washington Square Press Publication of Pocket Books, 1964), 42.

[12] Tiffany and Ringe, 68.

[13] See Matthew 1:5.

[14] See *The HarperCollins Study Bible* (New York: HarperCollins Publishers, 1993), 409, and Katherine Dob Sakenfeld Ruth (Louisville: John Knox Press, 1999), 7-9.

[15] *The HarperCollins Study Bible* , 409.

[16] "The Book of Ruth," *The New Interpreter's Bible* (Nashville: Abingdon Press, 1998), Volume II, 891.
[17] Ibid.
[18] Ibid., 892.
[19] See *The New Interpreter's Bible*, 901, and Michael E. Williams, editor *The Storyteller's Companion to the Bible: Volume Four: Old Testament Women* (Nashville: Abingdon Press, 1993), 116.
[20] See Numbers 25:1-2.
[21] *The HarperCollins Study Bible: New Revised Standard Version* (San Francisco: HarperCollins, 1993), 410-11.
[22] In the Jewish Midrash of *Ruth Rabbah,* Ruth's speech reflects a conversation that omits Naomi's responses. See Michael E. Williams, editor, *The Storyteller's Companion to the Bible: Volume Four: Old Testament Women* (Nashville: Abingdon Press, 1993), 114.
[23] Ibid, 111ff.
[24] Jim Goad. *The Redneck Manifesto* (New York: Touchstone, 1997), 35.
[25]See Matt Wray and Annalee Newitz, eds. *White Trash: Race and Class in America,* New York: Routledge, 1997), 5.
[26] Ibid.
[27] Walter Wink. *The Powers That Be: Theology for a New Millennium.* (New York: Doubleday, 1998), 164.
[28] Ibid.
[29] David Cantwell and Bill Friskics-Warren, *Heartaches by the Number: Country Music's 500 Greatest Singles* (Vanderbilt University Press and Country Music Foundation Press, 2003), 43.
[30] http://ourlyrics.host.sk/lyrics/nick_cave/nick_caveknoxville_girl.php.

Made in the USA
Lexington, KY
10 April 2014